ESCAPE FROM PLANET ALCATRAZ

BEYOND THE FURTHEST STAR

BY MICHAEL DAHL

ILLUSTRATED BY PATRICIO CLAREY

Raintree is an imprint of Capstone Global Library Limited, a company incorporated in England and Wales having its registered office at 264 Banbury Road, Oxford, OX2 7DY – Registered company number: 6695582

www.raintree.co.uk
myorders@raintree.co.uk

Edited by Aaron J. Sautter
Designed by Kay Fraser
Original illustrations © Capstone Global Library Limited 2021
Production by Tori Abraham
Originated by Capstone Global Library Ltd

978 1 4747 9319 3

British Library Cataloguing in Publication Data
A full catalogue record for this book is available from the British Library.

Acknowledgements
Design elements: Shutterstock: Agustina Camilion, A-Star, Dima Zel, Draw_Wing_Zen, Hybrid_Graphics, Metallic Citizen

Printed and bound in India.

CONTENTS

ERRO

PLATEAU of LENG

PHANTOM FOREST

POISON SEA

VULCAN MOUNTAINS

LAKE of GOLD

METAL MOON

DIAMOND MINES

MONSTER ZOO

ITS OF NO RETURN

PRISON STRONGHOLDS

SWAMP OF FLAME

SCARLET JUNGLE

PRISON ENERGY DRIVES

SPACE PORT
SONER INTAKE

ABYSS OF GIANTS

ZAK

THE PRISONERS

ZAK NINE

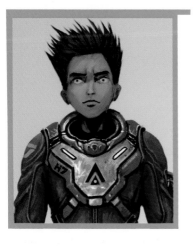

Zak is a teenage boy from Earth Base Zeta. He dreams of piloting a star fighter one day. Zak is very brave and is a quick thinker. But his enthusiasm often leads him into trouble.

ERRO

Erro is a teenage furling from the planet Quom. He has the fur, long tail, sharp eyes and claws of his species. Erro is often impatient with Zak's reckless ways. But he shares his friend's love of adventure.

THE PRISON PLANET

Alcatraz . . . there is no escape from this terrifying prison planet. It's filled with dungeons, traps, endless deserts and other dangers. Zak Nine and his alien friend, Erro, are trapped here. They had sneaked onto a ship hoping to see an awesome space battle. But the ship landed on Alcatraz instead. Now they have to work together if they ever hope to escape!

ZAK'S STORY . . . ESCAPE TO THE STARS >>>

Two days ago Erro and I rescued another prisoner from a deadly drone attack. To thank us, he took us with him to find a hidden spacecraft. Now we're flying away, and we'll soon escape Alcatraz for good. But the stars look very strange. . . . >>>>

CHAPTER ONE:
THE STARSHIP

Our starship rises quietly from the ground. The higher we get, the more I can see of Alcatraz.

"I cannot believe we are truly leaving this place," says Erro.

"We haven't left yet," I tell him. "Five more minutes, then we can turn on the thrusters."

When the thrusters hit full blast, we'll really move! That's when we can say we're escaping.

"Four more minutes," says Ozosh.

Ozosh is a prisoner from the desert planet Fleem. He looks just like a little elephant.

When we rescued Ozosh, he told us about this starship. He had heard some guards talking about it. We found it hidden deep in a swampy jungle.

"Is anyone following us, Erro?" I ask.

Erro is watching a small screen. It'll show him if any ships are following us.

"Negative," he says. "But that seems strange. Why don't the guards see us on their radar?"

"I don't care," I say. "I just want to get out of here."

"One more minute," says Ozosh.

"Wait!" says Erro suddenly. "Something *is* following us!"

CHAPTER TWO:
THE MISSILE

"Turn on the thrusters!" I shout.

"But we still have thirty seconds –"
says Ozosh, waving his big ears.

"Doesn't matter!" I cut him off.
"They've already seen us!"

I run back to my seat. I buckle in just
as Ozosh pushes a control button.

ZZZZWOOOOOOSSHHH!

Our starship races into space.

"Watch out!" shouts Erro.

Ozosh quickly steers the ship out of the way.

SSSHHRROOOOMM!

A big missile roars past our ship.

"They're trying to shoot us out of the sky!" Ozosh shouts.

"Can't this heap go any faster?" I ask.

CHAPTER THREE:
BEHIND THE MOON

VVRRRROOOOOOSHHH!

Another missile barely misses us.

BA-DOOOM!

"What was that?" Erro shouts.

"The first missile exploded," I say.

"That's strange," says Ozosh.
"I thought I just saw–"

Duh-Duh-Duh-Duh!

Shock waves from the explosion hit our ship. We all hold on tight until the ship stops shaking.

"I do not think we can outrun their weapons," says Erro.

"We need some protection," I say. Through the window I see a round object not far away.

"There! Head for that moon!" I tell Ozosh.

Erro and I once visited a metal moon above Alcatraz. I wonder if this one is made of metal too. I hope it can help protect us from the missiles.

Ozosh hits a few buttons with his elephant-like trunk. The ship heads towards the moon.

VVRRRROOOOOOSHHH!

A third missile streaks past our ship.

"Get us behind that moon!" I shout.

CHAPTER FOUR:
THE SIZE OF STARS

Ozosh flies the ship behind the moon. Then we head for the stars.

The moon is between our ship and the planet. The missiles shouldn't hit us now.

"Good thinking–" says Erro.

KRA-KOOOOMMMM!

Oh no! I was wrong. The third missile
still followed us. It exploded nearby.

"That was too close," Erro says, holding his ears.

"No kidding!" I agree.

Then I see Erro staring through the porthole. He has a funny look on his face.

"What's wrong now?" I ask.

"The stars," he says. "Look at the stars."

"I have a bad feeling about this," says Ozosh.

I hadn't noticed the stars before.

I was busy worrying about the missiles.

And the moon.

But now I see what Erro means.

The stars seem very close. And they look strange. They don't look like little points of light in the sky.

Instead, the stars are small glowing balls. They look like lamps.

CHAPTER FIVE:
ALCATRAZ

"Slow us down," I tell Ozosh.

He slows the ship to a crawl.

We float past the weird balls of light.

"The stars . . . they are not real,"
whispers Erro.

There are no more stars ahead of us,
either. Only darkness.

Another missile soars past us.

It quickly explodes.

KA-BOOOOOM!

Duh-Duh-Duh-Duh!

We hold on tight as the ship shakes.

And then we all see it. The truth is
shown in the light of the explosion.

Our ship is facing a giant metal wall.
The missile hit the wall and exploded.

"We are not in the universe!" says Erro. His eyes are wide with fear.

I shake my head. "I don't believe it," I say.

"There is no escape," says Ozosh gloomily.

Then I realize the truth. Alcatraz, its sun, its moons – and us. We're all inside the *real* prison.

We're trapped inside a globe the size of a solar system!

My head explodes with anger.

"But we flew to Alcatraz somehow!"
I yell. "We landed there in a ship!"

"There must be a way out," says Erro.

"And we're going to find it!" I shout.
"We have to!"

But we need to find it fast. The prison
guards will be coming for us soon. . . .

GLOSSARY

globe round, hollow sphere

missile explosive weapon that flies towards a target

negative another word meaning "no" or "not"

porthole small, round window in the side of a ship

radar device that uses radio waves to track the location of objects

shock wave strong burst of quickly moving air or water caused by an explosion

species group of living things that share similar features

thruster small rocket attached to a spacecraft that gives it extra power

universe everything that exists, including the planets, moons, stars and all of space

THINK ABOUT IT

1. In this story Zak and Erro are travelling with an alien that looks like a small elephant. Do you think other aliens could look like creatures from Earth? Talk about how your favourite animals might look and act if they were aliens from different planets.

2. To try to get away from the missiles, the boys fly behind a nearby moon. Can you think of another way they could have avoided the missiles? Describe what you would do if you were in their place.

3. Zak and Erro discover that Planet Alcatraz is inside another structure. How is this possible? How big would the structure need to be to hold a planet?

WRITE ABOUT IT

1. Write a short story that takes place before this adventure. Describe how the boys met Ozosh and how they got the ship.

2. Write a description of the structure that holds Planet Alcatraz. Explain what you think the real secrets are to keep people from escaping the prison planet.

ABOUT THE AUTHOR

Michael Dahl is the author of more than 300 books for young readers, including the Library of Doom series. He is a huge fan of Star Trek, Star Wars and Doctor Who. He has a fear of closed-in spaces, but has visited several prisons, dungeons and strongholds, both ancient and modern. He made a daring escape from each one. Luckily, the guards still haven't found him.

ABOUT THE ILLUSTRATOR

Patricio Clarey was born in 1978 in Argentina. He graduated in fine arts at the School of Visual Arts Martín Malharro, specializing in illustration and graphic design. Patricio currently lives in Barcelona, Spain, where he works as a freelance graphic designer and illustrator. He has created several comics and graphic novels, and his work has been featured in several books and other publications.